MY ANTIFA LOVER

A Riot of the Heart

Jessica Stranger

Copyright © 2020 Jessica Stranger

All rights reserved

The characters and events portrayed in this book are fictitious. Any similarity to real persons, living or dead, is coincidental and not intended by the author.

No part of this book may be reproduced, or stored in a retrieval system, or transmitted in any form or by any means, electronic, mechanical, photocopying, recording, or otherwise, without express written permission of the publisher.

CONTENTS

Title Page
Copyright
Chapter No. 1 — 1
Chapter No. 2 — 7
Chapter No. 3 — 15
Chapter No. 4 — 23
Chapter No. 5 — 30
Chapter No. 6 — 39
Chapter No. 7 — 47
Chapter No. 8 — 57
Chapter No. 9 — 66
Chapter No. 10 — 74

CHAPTER NO. 1

Alexandra's Point Of View:

How could I describe the feeling that I felt right now? It was not possible. Chris was nowhere to be seen and I was lost. There was misery everywhere. I saw fire all around me. Maybe this was the end of a beautiful beginning. And it was so weird. When you know you are about to die, you think only about the things which matter the most to you. And right now, being a congresswoman. Having the responsibilities of people and legislations on my head. My family waiting for me at home. My mother and my brother. But I didn't think about them right now.
The only thing I thought about and the only thing that I was concerned about was him. Chris.

The man who made and ruined everything. The building was on fire right now. And I was trapped inside it with no way out. And I knew I will be burnt to ashes till the fire brigade arrives because the fire was spreading quickly. I just had one regret on my mind. I should have told him that I loved him. I should have let him know that I cared. That after doing all the work of the day, he was the last person I thought about before I went to sleep every night.

But all I did was create hurdles, break promises and tell him lies. And now when I die, he will never know the truth. The truth that he has become the most important person in my life in the past two months. I lied on the ground breathing in the smoke from the fire. Living the very last moments of my life as my tears slipped away like my heart. I just hope he knows somehow that I cared. And I hope he knows that I believe him.

Flashback to 2 months ago:

This was it. The big day has finally come. Today was the hearing of new legislation in a congress meeting. Everyone was going to be there and some new members were also joining who just got elected this year. I just hope everything goes well and there is no bad blood between anyone at the end of the meeting. Peter, Jackson, Michael and all the other fellow members were going to be there.

A new bill was going to be passed today which has been under discussion for the past month. A new law was going to be passed which was undertaking the issues of the divorce rate increasing day by day in America. Hopefully this step helps in decreasing the rates of divorce and helping the upcoming generations form a better life. The divorce rates were increasing up to 80% and this was nowhere a reliable source anymore for a safe and secure relationship. Anyways, I shrugged off all the thoughts in my brain and went into the meeting room after smoothing out my black skirt and sliding my hair down my face. Let this be a quick and easy meeting...

The meeting went well. After 57 minutes of talking and declaring new ideas and topics, the meeting finally came to an end. Everything went okay and new legislation was approved which will enforce in decreasing the rates of the growing divorces in America. The divorces which were mostly made by the husbands in the relationship as per research. And so the new law enforced the husband to pay one million dollars to his wife if he wants to divorce her. In this way both the man and the woman will think twice in settling down. And the husband will have to be serious and responsible in the relationship instead of taking it as a joke.

I agreed to this matter for the sake of upcoming generations and for personal reasons as well which I didn't want to think about right now.

After the meeting ended, the congress people went into public and answered some questions which the media was eager to ask. The rally was extremely wild. I haven't seen this big of a crowd since, well since never. I have never seen so many people at one place like this before. It took me fifteen whole minutes to figure out what was actually happening and how were we going to communicate to the public. I saw some banners saying weird things. And most of the crowd was filled with men, journalists and the people who belonged to different parts of media. Our head answered some questions which the journalists asked and as I stood behind, I noticed that most of the people were protestors of this new legislation.

Most of the boys had banners which said things like, "Equal rights for Men!", "Women can be Free but Men must pay One Million Dollars to be Free?", "I can Leave Someone Whenever I Want!", "Feminists Are Screwed!"

I furrowed my eyebrows when I realized how men were extremely against this law. I was informed that this would happen but not to this intensity. In head it seemed like no big deal. If you don't want to be with someone, don't marry them. And when you do marry them, you shouldn't just leave them like you just wanted a taste. You should be loyal to them. And all the boys protesting made me think that they were against this law because they wanted to screw whoever they liked. Marry whoever they wanted and leave the girl when she gets old and useless. My blood boiled when I thought about what had happened to my sister. Passing this bill had a big contribution to what had happened to my sister and I wasn't going back on this law no matter what.

My team and I answered questions like, "Do you think this law will actually help in decreasing the divorce rates? "Will there will be less marriages now due to this new law?", "Do you think this law is justified for men?"

The audience was also given a chance to speak and ask a few questions. Most of audience's questions were dismissed because of their unprofessional attitude and rough language and very few were answered by the congress team. I was so glad I was standing behind a deck because my legs were literally shaking from seeing so many people at one place like this. Even though they were restrained behind a fence and were being overlooked by security but still I always felt afraid of huge crowds. It wasn't even that huge but I was still scared of it. It gave me goosebumps every five minutes.

The mic was passed on to another person in the crowd who wanted to ask a question. My eyes immediately noticed his piercing blue eyes and black cap. He had a dark green loose jacket on and I swear even hiding behind that cap, his eyes didn't fail to catch my attention.

"Miss Alexandria my question is directed to you." He started to speak, and as soon as his eyes landed on me I somehow forgot about all of the crowd. It was like we were the only two people in the hall. His eyes had so much depth in them that I felt like I could never hide from his gaze even if I tried. They were accusing, haunting, mesmerizing and somehow I felt insecure under his gaze. "Would you have passed this bill if you ever a man?" He accused me with his eyes more than his words and my breath got caught in between my throat as his question settled in my mind.

Would I have favored this legislation if I was a guy? My mind comprehended the question over and over again and his determining eyes never left my face. I swallowed the air in my throat and my eyes tried to hide from his. His gaze was the most intimidating thing I have ever seen in my life.

"Next question!" The reporters moved to another person when I didn't answer thinking I have dismissed the question like many others. But I didn't ignore it. I was thinking

5

about it and I realized that I have never thought of it like that before.

Another question was being asked by someone but his eyes stayed glued to my face. I tried to avert my gaze and stare at the person currently asking a question but my eyes kept averting back to that particular stranger's face. He had a light smirk on his face which I noticed the third time I averted my gaze back to him in the overloading crowd.

And that damn devilish smirk made me hate him all the more. Hope he never comes to another rally again or I'll have to slap that devilish smile off of his face myself.

CHAPTER NO. 2

It was a weird and unsettling feeling that I couldn't shake off. I have been trying to take my mind of off the events that happened three days ago. But I wasn't succeeding in any situation. The situation in congress and the situation in my mind. I already knew I wasn't in favor of the law that passed three days ago in that big meeting. But I didn't know I'd feel so guilty like this afterwards. Why did I not feel this way before? I couldn't figure out any answer to my questions.

But one thing I was sure of. It was his question. His question made me think all over again about what I was doing in my life. I had this big position and huge responsibility on my head but I acted like it was no big deal.

It was all so frustrating. I sighed and looked in the mirror. A pale and somewhat sun tinted face stared back at me. With her dark black eyes looking like they could kill with their looks if they wanted to. Her dark brown hair slipped down her shoulders in light waves and collar bones were as visible as day. She seemed like a powerful yet insecure woman when you carefully looked into her eyes. And that powerful yet insecure woman was me.

It was 3:44 P.M and I had the day off. Most of the times my off days were the time for me to relax and catch up on sleep but today I wasn't able to sleep or relax at all. My mind was racing with unwelcomed thoughts and I wasn't able to do anything about it. Giving up I got ready in simple clothes to go to my favorite place which always took my mind off of all the things.

I changed into a light blue T-shirt and white cardigan with dark brown jeans. I wore one of my most comfortable sneakers and tied my hair into a loose ponytail and few locks of my hair fell on my face. And I was ready to go.

I reached there in twenty minutes. It was my most favorite and secret place which I came to visit occasionally when I had spare time. It was a very old forest at the back of my childhood school and I remember going there every time I got the chance. And now I was a fully grown woman but still, I could picture my ten-year-old self coming here and enjoying the quiet atmosphere.

I drove myself because I didn't know how long I was going to stay and I didn't want to keep my driver waiting. I walked through the woods and remembered all the ways and the trees that I claimed as a child. This was something no one could take away from me and it gave me eternal peace.

I walked for more than half an hour and finally reached the small lake that my eyes desired to see. Sun was slowly setting and it created a dazzling glow on the clear water. I stood by the lake and turned my eyes towards the sun and closed them, taking in all the warmth of the passing summer. Fall was just around the corner waiting for summer to complete its course.

Suddenly I heard creaking and rustling of bushes behind me. I quickly opened my eyes and turned to look in that direction. But all I saw were trees and broken branches. I turned my face back and stared ahead at the lake. Maybe it's the wind blowing. But my thoughts were proven wrong when I heard the voice again and this time when I turned around someone was approaching.

At first, I didn't recognize him, but when he slowly came closer my mind flashed-back to those intense blue eyes eating me up at the rally. He still had that light slap able smirk on his face and my heart suddenly started to beat a thousand miles per minute.

"Good evening." He said, his voice was deep and husky. And now without a microphone, it seemed more real.

"Good evening." I greeted back, unable to comprehend what to say to him. Is he here to have the answer to his question?

"Enjoying the very few last sunsets of summer?" He asked coming closer to stand next to me by the lake.

I was taken back by his smooth and relaxed posture. I immediately knew who he was just by looking at those intense blue eyes but still, I wanted to confirm, "You're one of the protestors at the rally that happened three days ago right?"

"Yes." He replied nodding. I stared at him uneasily because

I didn't know why he was here or if he had been following me this whole time.

He smiled slowly when I didn't say something more, "Don't worry. I'm not here to repeat my question again and neither was I stalking you. I happen to come here often on Mondays and Fridays. And seeing you here is a coincidence." He said.

I smiled back at him and nodded. Not really sure how to proceed with the conversation I stared back at the lake ignoring him. Hoping he might leave on his own. But he stood there silently beside me, staring ahead at the sunset.

"Alexandria right?" He asked after five minutes.

"Mmm-hmm." I hummed in response hoping he would get the notion and leave me alone.
Instead, I heard his chuckle.

How dare he!

I stared at him from the corner of my eyes to notice what he was laughing about but I couldn't find any specific reason.

Maybe he is just mad.

Yes, I'll believe that.

"I'm Corner Smith." He extended his hand out for me to shake. I shook his hand out of curtsey without looking at him.

"It's great weather today." He tried to start the conversation again.

I full-on ignored him. "Hmmm…"

He stayed quiet for another two minutes before speaking. "You looked great by the way, standing on that stage."

My blood started to boil to a thousand degrees. What does he mean I looked great? I was standing there to serve a purpose. Because I have the responsibility of the law upon my goddamn head and all he cares about is me looking good on the stage?

I turned to face him and hopefully teach him a lesson. "Is that all you boys care about? The girl looking good and sexy on the stage?" Venom was dripping from my voice as I spoke those words.

I heard him laugh fully at my words.

"Are you serious?" He asked once he calmed down his laughs to think about what I said.

I stared at him dead on, which indicated I was damn serious about what I said.

"You know very well, what I care about Alexandria." He said with the same serious tone he used when he asked his question at the rally.

"I'm not interested in what you care about; so can you please leave?" I said. I was done with him and his laughs and his hypnotizing blue eyes. I wanted to clear my head full of rummaging thoughts not to fill it with his useless banter.

"Yeah, no worries. I'm sorry I bothered you." He finally said the words I wanted to hear. But as soon as he said them, my heart dropped with loneliness. It felt like it needed company and I was providing it with only silence which wasn't helping in any way.

I saw him put his head down and turn around to leave. I stared at his broad back as he took steps away from me. And each passing step increased my heartbeat by the minute.

"Wait," I said out of nowhere. It was the first I spoke from my heart instead of listening to my head.

I saw him stop in his heels and slowly turn around. He had a serious look in his eyes and the slight smile he always has on his lips was nowhere to be found. "I'm sorry. I shouldn't have behaved like that." I said what my heart wanted me to say while my mind screamed at me not to apologize to him.

His light smile immediately returned and he came back to stand beside me. My heart somehow did a somersault when I realized that I was the cause of that smile.

"It's okay. I also have my rough days." He said looking down at me. He was probably four to five inches taller than me and I was 5:4 feet.

"It's just hard to clear your head sometimes," I told him honestly. "I have been having this trouble for a while now." Words automatically started to flow out of my mouth, letting him know how I felt.

"Have you tried talking to someone about it?" He said putting his hands inside his jeans pockets.

I furrowed my eyebrows thinking about his question. "No. I actually haven't." I said, surprised at the answer myself.

"Well maybe instead of silence, you could try talking to someone about it." He said.

I looked up into his mesmerizing blue eyes and admired how the sunset glow fell upon his dark hair that wasn't covered with a cap right now.

"I could try that," I said. "Can I ask something?"

"Yes." He immediately answered.

"Why are you trying to actually help me?

He seemed perplexed for a moment at my words. Then his eyebrows relaxed and he said, "Because you're the first normal congress person I have seen in my life." He said. And somehow his answer made me smile unconsciously.

"You don't know me. I could be far from normal." I teased.

He smiled and I noticed that a dimple formed on his left cheek whenever he smiled deeply. "Well, I could find that out." He replied.

"I honestly thought you'd hate me because you were one of the protestors." I honestly said.

"From what I've learned, you shouldn't hate the person but the bad deed that they do." He said.
I thought about his words for a second and I couldn't deny that he was right. He was charming and wise...

~~~~~~~~~~~~~~

I went home that day feeling something I have never felt before. He was right. Instead of silence, I actually needed someone with whom I could talk to. It was a very unexpected meeting but I don't regret it one bit.

He gave me his number and said to call him if I ever needed someone to talk to. In my head, I knew I'd never actually call him but my heart deep down said otherwise. I decided to fold that piece of paper in the pocket of my cardigan and let it rest as long as I didn't need it.

That night, curiosity didn't let me sleep. One thing was running on my mind which was Corner Smith. I had to know who this mysterious stranger was and why he suddenly decided to pop into my life out of nowhere. Maybe it's some type of miracle but the logical side of my mind forced me to investigate. I called some people and told them to find information on a person named Corner Smith. Being a congresswoman did have its perks you know.

If I don't find something suspicious or crazy about him I'd just assume he was a miracle sent from God. I just hope the things I fear don't come true.

CHAPTER NO. 3

It has been ten days. Ten days since the meeting with that fallen angel that decided to show up in my life. His eyes were imprinted in my mind. His voice echoed in my ears at night. His smile was so contagious that I smiled just remembering it.

It was so weird because I have never felt this way before in my life ever. Or maybe I was always too busy to actually think about things like these. I sat in my office and thought about him while I stared at the printed paper in my hand. The bill was passed by the congress even with all of the protestors claiming to take it back. And the bill was currently under review of the Senate. If the Senate approved it, then nobody can stop this law from taking place.

My inner voice told me to do something about it. To fight for the people and do what feels right. I had the power of speaking up and I knew few people would also come on my side when I raise my voice against this act. But I was hesitant. I was scared of what could happen.

The person who was leading this whole legislation was

Benedict Wilbur. He wanted the police gone and he was doing everything he can to make sure it happens. He was the head of the congress house, the person with supreme power and I was afraid to go against him. But ever since the bill was passed and given under the review of the Senate, my conscience didn't let me sleep at night. Thoughts and feelings haunted me, willing me to do something about it before it's too late.

I rubbed my forehead which was starting to hurt right now and throw the printed paper on my desk. I leaned back in my chair and closed my eyes. The fight of my head and heart was real and I needed to do something about it.

I thought about the piece of paper in my cardigan's pocket waiting for me. He said to give him a call anytime I need someone to talk to. Maybe I should try talking to someone. I thought about all of my school friends whom I lost as soon as I joined politics. I didn't have time and space for anyone in my life back then and people who were once close to me slowly started to drift away. My family was currently settled in Nashville while I moved to Seattle following the demands of my work. I learned that ultimately you reach a point in your life in which you have to choose between your family and your work. And that same thing happened to me. On one hand, I succeeded in getting elected as a congresswoman, on the other hand, I became extremely lonely. It was a blessing and a curse at the same time.

I willed my conscience to calm down and promised to do something about this new law tomorrow. I just knew I had to. It was a feeling I could not ignore.

I went home at 8:30 P.M and got freshened up. I ordered Chinese food and turned on the T.V. It was my daily routine. Coming back to an empty house, ordering food, turning the T.V just to fill the silent house with some noise, eat and stare at the T.V until sleep hits me and then drag myself to bed and sleep. This was my life. Lonely and alone. Sometimes I talked to my family on the phone. I had my mother and my little brother who just joined college. I missed both of them. I also missed Monty, my cat. My family adopted her when I was 13 years old but I couldn't bring her with me to Seattle because I knew I won't be able to take care of her. I was always on duty and looking after a pet was didn't compromise with my schedule.

I sighed and stared at the ceiling. What a wonderful life. I thought sarcastically. Just when you think you have everything you ever wanted, it proves to be totally wrong. I don't know what I want any more from life.

After eating the food, I decided to turn the T.V off and read a book for a change. I went into my room and grabbed a romance book which in normal circumstances I would never read. But these past few days have been far from normal so I decided to give it a shot. I laid in my bed and opened the first page.

I was on page no. 34 when I started to hear strange noises getting louder slowly. I closed the book and blinked a few times thinking that I might be imagining things but I still kept hearing them. I got up and sat on my bed. The sounds were becoming clearer and clearer each passing second making me more puzzled. As the noise became more clear I realized they were voices of people. The voices you would hear from a crowd. I got up and opened the door to my balcony to look outside. It was currently 12:20 A.M in the morning. What were people doing outside so late? I looked out and saw a big crowd of people just a few feet away from my house. They were coming towards it and my eyes widened when I realized they were protestors.

I saw them holding banners and sticks and some I even saw having guns in their hand. I ran back inside the house and closed the balcony door. My heart raced like it was about to explode and I felt like I couldn't breathe. I knew the security was at the main gate and they would probably call for backup but... Shit! It seemed like the end. It seemed like the crowd I saw at the rally. Shit! Is...is Corner leading them? He was one of the protestors of this law. And he was standing between them at the rally too. Is he leading his pack and planning on killing me tonight because I didn't favor him in any way. How dare he! And here I was thinking about calling him and...yes! I will fucking call him. And let him know how much he has hurt me with his actions.

I ran and stumbled towards my closet to grab the cardigan which had his number in it. I realized my hands were shaking and a scream escaped my lips from terror when I heard the first rock being thrown at my window. With shaking hands, I took the piece of paper out and dialed his number. How dare he do this to me? I was just starting to trust him and he was doing this to me?
Tears fell from my eyes and I put my ringing phone on my ear waiting for him to pick up so I can say my final words to

him. He picked up on the twelfth ring.

"Hello?" His voice seemed slacked and tired. And I didn't hear any background noise like I was hearing from down the road.

"I fucking hate you, Corner Smith!" I cried. "You ruined my fucking life and you don't even know it! I was trying to be better, t-trying to d-do the right thing b-but... you never bothered to give me a chance, did you?! I hope you die somewhere in a ditch! I hope no one ever loves you! You didn't even let me try!" I cried and screamed and sobbed and stuttered on the phone and ignored his confused whats and groans. He didn't do me justice and he would pay for it one day.

I shut the phone and threw it on my bed. Just as I was about to back away further from the window currently being smashed with rocks, I heard the sound of a gunshot and the next thing I knew the whole glass door of my balcony shattered in pieces. The broken pieces flew towards me from the force of the shot and I barely had enough time to cover myself with my arms. The pieces pierced the skin of my hands and arms and I backed away till my back hit the wall behind me and I slid down giving up on everything.

Maybe this was how I was supposed to die. This was the result of doing things that your conscience tells you not to do. I was devastated at myself and the life I choose. And for the first time in my life, I thought about who will miss me when I die. My mom and my little brother will find out over the news that I died from the protestors attack. And they will be heartbroken. But other than them, there was no one who would miss me. No one's life would be that affected by my death. These were the qualities of staying lonely.

I sat on the floor watching unable to move and watched the devastating scene in front of me. I don't know how much time passed but I sat there. Hearing the sounds of sirens, noises of people shouting, I wouldn't be surprised if they set the house on fire right now. My eyes closed and opened as blood dripped down my arms and hands. I tried to take the shards out but I couldn't bring myself to inflict any more pain. I just hoped that a bullet would come flying and hit me in my chest so all of this agony is finally over.

Dropping in and out of consciousness, I felt like I was dreaming the whole incident. Especially the familiar voice that I heard speaking in what sounded like a microphone. The sound was loud enough for me to hear but my mind wasn't able to focus on what the voice was saying. I heard the voice speak for God knows how long and the pain in my arms and hands increased every passing minute. I needed to get the shards out but I could barely keep my eyes open. It was like I was breathing but no air was coming in my lungs.

After a few more minutes, I heard the sound of a door opening nearby with my eyes closed. My eyelids felt too heavy to open them and I felt like sleeping. I heard footsteps approaching near me and then an alarming voice say, "Alexandria?!" I was too tired to answer yes to the voice. "Alexandria!" I felt someone gently grab my face and yell my name way too close to my ear. I wanted to sleep right now not be yelled at.

I squinted my heavy eyelids open and tried to frown angrily at the face to show my distress. I thought I was dreaming this too. It was Corner. His face was so close and his eyes were so deep that I could drown in them. I still managed to frown and pout and say, "Can't yuh see em trying tuh sleep?" I slurred, tired out of my wits. I saw him smile with sadness in his eyes before I closed my eyes again.

The only thing which didn't let me drift into darkness was the throbbing pain in my arms and hands. It made me realize I was still alive and in agony. I just wanted to end it all. I was too tired to fight anyone anymore.

"I'm so sorry..." I heard the voice speak and then I felt like I was floating in the air as I was picked up from the cold floor and into a warm pair of arms. I groaned in pain as my right arm scratched against something but I didn't have the ability to open my eyes and tell him. After walking a few more steps, I was placed upon something soft. Way more soft and comfortable than the hard floor I was lying on for the past hour.

"Corner?" I murmured with my eyes closed, praying he'd hear me.

"Yes?" I heard him reply quickly. His voice seemed very close to my face.

"Tell them I was against the law..." I said what had been disturbing my mind for the month. And I didn't force myself to stay awake long enough to hear his reply. Maybe the message was meant more for him than the protestors down by the road. But either way, my conscience was finally at peace at admitting the truth to him...

CHAPTER NO. 4

I knew I was not in my house as soon as I got my senses back. I heard footsteps and hushed voices around me. I opened my eyes slowly, thankful that they weren't as heavy as before. A nurse was standing by my side with a doctor on my left. Shit! I was in the hospital. But why?

Slowly memories started to come back as a nightmare to me. The shouting, the voice of the crowd, window-smashing, someone speaking in a microphone, door slamming open and then…Corner. Corner was there. Panicked I looked quickly down to the foot of my bed and saw him. He was standing there with an unreadable expression on his face. When he saw me looking he smiled at me but that smile didn't reach his eyes. That smile wasn't the smile I saw at the lake in the forest when he talked to me.

He was the first face I recognized and it calmed me down a bit. But my anger increased when I realized that he was one of the protestors who led the crowd last night. I remember, I called him and cursed him out for not giving me a chance. I can't believe he had the nerve to come up to my house afterwards! I can't believe he has the nerve to stand in front of me like this! I fucking hate this man.

I stared daggers at him and if looks could kill, he'd be dead by now. I decided to stay quiet until the nurse and the doctor left. I noticed that the head of my security, Roddick was also standing in the far right corner of the room.

The nurse and the doctor introduced themselves as Dr Charlie and Susan. And told me about the cuts on my arms and hands. They were stitched up and wrapped in bandages so I couldn't see the wounds. But I felt them and thankfully they weren't hurting as bad as before. The doctor and the nurse left after checking a few things and measuring my blood pressure.

I still stared daggers at Corner as he slowly came and sat beside me. It made me aggravated all the more.

"How are you feeling?" He asked slowly.

"You seem quite relaxed after your plan failed in killing me," I said. My voice was extremely dry and husky. But I tried my best to let him know that I was going to fucking send him to jail soon for doing this.

The most unexpected thing happened after that.

I saw him chuckle.

Real genuine laugh.

And I frowned in confusion. Was there something wrong with his head?

"Are you absolutely out of your mind? It's no time for laughing. You should get your things ready for jail. I will file a report against you. You won't get away with this." I said more forcefully and angrily to make my point clear.

"Alexandria, I would never do anything to hurt you." He

quieted down and said with an impeccable voice. I almost believed him until I recalled again what he did to me last night.

"You protested against me last night!" I told him.

He smiled again. "I wasn't among the protestors that attacked your house Alexandria. I came after when you called me." He explained.

Fucking liar.

"You couldn't make up a better lie to save your sorry ass, could you?" I said with venom dripping from my voice. How dare he hurt me first then pretend like he did nothing wrong.

"I'm not lying." He said with that deep tone again that reached my soul.

I stared at him and he stared back at me. He was looking right into my eyes and I've heard that when people lie they never dare to look in the eye of the person they're lying to.

"Miss Preston, he is telling the truth. He was the person that stopped the protestors from attacking your house. And later took you to the hospital." Roddick said, stepping further from the right corner of the room. "I was with him the whole time. The crowd was getting out of our hands but he stopped them." What the hell was happening?! My mind was filled with so many thoughts that it was going to explode.

I stared back at Corner and he stared at me with that unfathomable expression on his stupid gorgeous face.

"Can you leave us alone for a moment?" I directed to Roddick. He nodded and went out, closing the door behind him.

"You actually saved me?" I asked him.

"You could say that." He replied. "I tried my best to reach there on time as soon as you called. But still...I..." He looked at my injured arms and hands with guilt written all over his face. "I'm sorry." He said turning his head down and my eyes immediately softened. He was the first person outside my family to actually care for me. And It was a weird feeling. I didn't want him to feel guilty for what happened to me.

"I'm okay. I should have stood further away from my window." I told him trying to take away his guilt. "Thank you for saving me," I said apologetically. I always get the wrong idea of the people first then they turn out to be a totally different person.

He smiled warmly back at me. "I'm glad you okay."

After three hours, the doctor and the nurse came back to let me know that I can go home whenever I want. My reports came back clear and nothing was threatening about my situation. The doctor told me a few precautions and medicines to relieve the pain and said it will take around a week before they can take the stitches out. I thanked them and decided to go home as soon as I could. I never liked hospitals and its atmosphere always made me nauseous.

I changed into normal clothes that thankfully the nurse provided and motioned Roddick to get the car ready.

"You're going home?" He asked even though he already knew I was.

"Yes," I replied. I had to rest and I should better head to a place more comfortable like my room. My room...Shit! I almost forgot. It was shattered and covered with broken glass. And all the horrible memories that were now attached to it. I stopped in the middle of grabbing the doorknob to get out and stared blankly. I can't go back there. What if the protestors come back? I never really knew my home would feel like the most unsafe place for me someday.

"What's wrong?" He asked as soon as he saw the troubled look on my face.

"I have to get my house repaired first before I go there," I told him sadly. Shrugging the horrible thoughts off I decided to choose a hotel for my temporary stay. "I'd have to look for a hotel," I told him finally going outside the door. He walked beside me as we went into the lobby to exit.

"You could stay with me until then." He said out of nowhere. I slowed in my tracks and looked at him.

"I'm serious. And besides someone should be there to take care of you until your wounds heal." He said. I looked up into his eyes which provided nothing but warmth to my soul. I knew I was fighting with myself so I wouldn't like him but I kept getting drawn to him. And his invitation seemed like a breath of fresh air to me. I didn't want to stay alone in a hotel room. And I couldn't go to live with my mother in Nashville because of my business requirements.

"Will that be okay?" He asked when I didn't reply. I quickly averted my gaze, hating myself for staring at him.

"Yeah, that'll be okay. But your family?" I asked, walking towards my car.

"I live alone." He told me. And the realization hit me that he might be just as lonely as I was in my life. I actually didn't know about his family at all. Maybe I could get to know him better till my time with him ends.

Roddick asked about where we would be going and I told him at Corner's place. He nodded and Corner gave him directions to his house.

For the first time in my life, everything was happening out of place. Going against my schedule felt so odd but I welcomed it. For the first time in my life, I wasn't worried about what would happen next or where would the unknown road lead me to. But I wasn't scared. And for the first time in my life, I wasn't alone either...

"This is my room." He gave me a tour of his small yet cozy house and finally we reached his room. It was normal in size and looked extremely comfortable. He has silk duvets on the bed, comfy sofas by the window, a small table with a laptop on it and a chair beside it.

"It looks extremely cozy," I told him the truth. He smiled.

"Why don't you lay down and rest for a while in my bed? I have another guest room in the house but it has been two years since it's been used. No one actually stays here except for me." He said. I stared at him with a weird feeling in my stomach. Why was I suddenly feeling so close to him? I had no idea. But It felt like he understood me even when I haven't told him anything.

I nodded and he left. I sat down on the bed and immediately felt the sleep hit me. I had been trying to keep myself together ever since the horrible incident and finally, now I could relax.

This was such a new feeling for me. Nobody took care of me like this before. I could sleep in this bed and have somebody look after me. I could rely on him. I could be with him. And he could be with me. I smiled at that thought. Being together. It felt so magical.

I laid down on the bed after taking off my sweater. My arms hurt a bit as I pulled the sleeves off and I bit my lower lip to stop the groans from escaping. This was going to be a long week until the wounds heal. I finally took a deep breath and laid on the bed getting comfortable. The smell of the bed oddly seemed familiar. I realized it was the same scent I felt last night when Corner carried me to the bed. I smiled at that realization and drifted off to sleep.

CHAPTER NO. 5

I woke up to the smell of eggs and burning toast. My eyes quickly popped open and my heart rate quickened as I realized it was not my room. Then it suddenly calmed down when I remembered that I was staying at Corner's house after all the horrible incidents happened. I looked through the curtains and saw the sun shining brightly in the blue sky. It was 7:30 A.M ticking on the wall clock. I remember I came back from the hospital yesterday around the time of evening. I can't believe I stayed asleep throughout the evening and night. I slept for at least 14 hours. I haven't slept this long since... well since never. I always woke up in the middle of the night for at least two to three times. But I have never slept like the dead before in my life.

I rubbed my eyes and looked at the bandages on my hands. I was still wearing the same clothes I changed into when I was at the hospital. I decided to freshen up and take the bandages off because the doctor said I could take them off after 12 hours. I went into the bathroom and slowly took off the band-aids. I noticed that the cuts weren't that deep except for two. It seemed like my right arm took all the shards. It had 7 to 8 stitches and my left arm only had three. And the rest of the cuts weren't that deep just small scratches. I thanked God and decided to take a shower and soak my wounds in warm water and soap. That always helped.

I went out of the bathroom and looked for some clothes I could wear. Corner was nowhere to be found so I went into his closet to look for some clothes. I hope he doesn't mind. I decided to wear an oversized grey T-shirt of his with a pair of shorts I found in the drawers. They looked worn out but comfy. Then I took an hour-long shower and slowly tended to wash my wounds with warm water and soap, careful not to pull on the stitches. Then I dried off and wore the clothes.

I looked at my reflection in the mirror and was completely taken off guard. I looked like a completely different person. The girl I always saw at my house in the mirror was not the girl that was looking at me right now. My face looked pale and soft and my dark circles were more visible than before. My wet hair fell around my shoulders in small waves and my lips were a little bit swollen. I haven't seen myself this untidy since my childhood days. When I use to run around in our backyard and play in the dirt with my little brother. Ever since I joined politics, I never stepped out of my circle. Never actually had fun and let myself lose. And never crossed any limits and boundaries that I created around myself.

But right now when I looked at the girl in the mirror, standing in that oversized grey t-shirt, worn out and hurt. I saw the reflection of that little girl in the backyard playing with her brother. She was not ladylike at all but she had a shining glint in her eyes that proved that she could do whatever she put her heart into. And for the first time in my life, I smiled at the reflection in the mirror and she smiled back at me. Tattered and worn out but somehow she was still happy than she had ever been.

I brushed my teeth and went out of the bedroom and into the dining room that Corner showed me yesterday. The smell of omelette was more pungent in the dining room. I took a few more steps, peaked around the kitchen and saw him. His back was turned towards me indicating that he didn't know about my presence. I watched him work and take the eggs out of the frying pan and into two plates. I thought I heard him hum a song too. It unconsciously placed a smile upon my face. I knocked on the door to made my presence known.

He seemed a little surprised when he heard the knock but quickly turned around and smiled at me, "Good morn'in!" He greeted. I came inside the kitchen and greeted him back. It was the first time in many years that someone was there to greet me in the morning. For a second he kept staring at me. He looked down and then up, and he had a very serious expression on his face. I thought I had offended him in some way. Then I figured he was probably looking at the clothes that I was wearing.

"I borrowed your clothes. I hope you don't mind. I wanted to take a shower and didn't have anything else." I said unconsciously tugging on his t-shirt and nervously staring at him.

I saw a depth in his eyes and after hearing my words he quickly averted his gaze and looked back on the plates that he was preparing. "No no. It's fine." I heard him say.

After a few seconds of silence, I decided to change the subject, "It smells delicious!" I exclaimed looking at the food in the plates.

"It's the first time I made breakfast for two. It took me a little while." He was blushing at my compliment. I chuckled and grabbed the plates from the counter and placed them on the table in the dining room. He also fried bacon and made toasts. My mouth was literally watering. I haven't eaten in like twenty hours.

"I made a lot of food because I figured you would be very hungry since you didn't eat anything at the hospital either." He said as we both sat down after placing all the food on the table. My eyes were shining from seeing all of the food and I couldn't wait to dig in.

"I'm famished!" I exclaimed. I couldn't wait to stuff all of the food in my mouth.

I saw him laugh out loud at my words and expressions and we both starting to eat. The food was incredibly good. My cooking skills were nowhere near his. The only good thing I could make was coffee or tea. I was literally stuffing my mouth after one bit and another and I saw him suppress his laughter at my eating expressions. What could I do? I was very hungry.

We finished off the food and I slid back. I was full and relaxed, it was the first time that this happened in my life. His smile was still present on his lips and I quietly admired it from afar.

"I'm glad you enjoyed the food." He and we both got up to put the dishes away. "How's your hand?" Looking down at my hands and arms.

"Thankfully they are not as bad," I said. "I opened the bandages and most of the stitches are done on one arm." I pointed at it. "And the rest are scratches," I said.

He nodded, "I'm glad. I got very scared last night when I saw you on the floor like that." He spoke and grabbed the dishes from my hands and placed them on the counter.

"I'm glad you were there to help me out. I don't know what I would have done without your help." I told him honestly. I genuinely don't know. I grabbed another pair of dishes from the table and was going to put them in the sink when he grabbed them in the middle of my way and gave me a look.

"What?" I said when he gave the look.

"Sit down. I'm not letting you do any work around here." He said and turned around with the empty plates in his hand.

"I can't just sit around for two days. You've already helped me enough. Besides, I'll get bored." I said following him into the kitchen.

"We could do lots of other things, so you won't get bored." He said without turning around. He had started the faucet and was washing the dishes now.

"Like what?" I pouted and stared up at him.

"Like watch movies, play games, take walks around the forest behind the school." He said and glanced at me from the corner of his eyes when he mentioned the forest behind the school.

"And how would I help you?" I said to him.

"By sitting down and taking care of yourself." He required. I rolled my eyes, giving up on him and went to sit on the living room couch. His sofas were extremely soft and cushioned. I could get used to living here. I waited for him to come back and turned the T.V on to keep myself busy. He appeared after ten minutes, wiping his hands on a white towel.

"Enjoying T.V?" He asked when he saw me staring at the T.V and ignoring him.

"Yeah." I lied. I was actually waiting for him but I didn't want him to know that.

"What are you watching?" He sat beside me on the couch and stared ahead. "A documentary about squirrels?" He laughed.

I frowned, "What's wrong with squirrels?" I said.

"Nothing. I just…You were looking at the T.V like you were seeing something very important." He replied suppressing his laughter.

"Squirrels are also important." I tried to stay mad but it was so hard because his dimple kept showing, making my heart melt.

"Well you keep watching these squirrels, I will head-on and make some calls." He said, getting up from the couch and going into his bedroom. My heart immediately saddened again but I remembered that it was Saturday so he won't necessarily be going to his work. I suddenly remembered that a big conference meeting was going to happen on Monday. In which some questions were going to be answered and all the congress people were going to attend. I also had to be there. Shit! Why does it have to be so soon? I bit my nails and thought about what would happen that day. I had anxiety just thinking about it. I decided to shake these thoughts off for now and focus on the damn squirrels on the T.V. I just needed to stay calm and be ready for whatever happens…

Corner and I stayed together for the rest of the day and I called Roddick and told him to bring my mobile phone and other necessities like some clothes from my home so I could live here. I also told him to bring my toothbrush because I had to use Corner's for today. I hope he never finds out about it.

We talked about everything and nothing as we laid on the couch and watched mindless T.V. I asked him about his occupation and he told me that he worked as an assistant director in some marketing company and he lived away from his family due to business reasons. He said he was always traveling from place to place and that is why he mostly ended up alone. That was the main reason why he knew how to cook very well too.

I also told him about my life and how hectic it got sometimes. I told him about my family living in Nashville and how I had to move away from them and settle into Seattle. I realized while talking to him that we both lived very lonely lives and somehow that made our bond stronger.

"I wanted to ask you one thing," I told him. It was almost night time and we were eating grapes while sitting beside the window on cushioned chairs which were made in the shape of giant hands.

"Shoot." He said popping another grape in his mouth.

"How did you stop the protestors from attacking my house? From what I remember they weren't going to stop at any costs until they had my blood." I asked him the question which was running through my mind all day.

"You didn't hear?" He asked sitting straight up.

"No," I replied.

"I told them that you were actually in favor of them and were going to help eliminate the law. I used a microphone and convinced them that you were on our side. And they believed me since I'm a protestor myself." He slowly explained.

"But how did you know I was going to do that?" I asked baffled.

"I didn't." He simply stated.

I gave him an are-you-for-real look and he decided to clarify further.

"I had to stop them in some way Alexandria. I knew you were up there and I would have done anything to save you." He spoke in a clear tone.

My heart felt so weird at that revelation that someone actually cared for me that much. "I'm really sorry about cursing you out on the phone." I needed to apologize after all he had done for me.

"I'm actually glad you did." He chuckled, "I was waiting for you to call me ever since we parted ways at the lake. I'm happy you did even when it was only for cursing me out." He said making me smile.

"Thank you for everything," I told him.

And we proceeded to eat grapes in silence.

"Are you going to speak up about the bill at the conference happening on Monday." He asked after some time.

"I'm thinking about it," I said honestly. There was no reason to hide anything from him now.

"I think you should if your inner voice tells you to." His face in dim light seemed more serious and it was hard not to listen to him. "I will help you in any way I can. I just don't want our homeland to feel like an unsafe place." He explained with sadness and depth in his voice.

I nodded because I agreed with him, "I know. I was never in favor of it since the beginning but I never said anything. I think It's time I let my voice be heard. Maybe it'll make a difference." I was hurt and broken down but I have never felt more powerful now that I was finally listening to my inner voice.

I didn't care if it made a difference or not. But I knew my conscience would be at peace once I do the things that I was meant to do and fight for people's rights. And this time I also had an impeccable gentleman with me. What could possibly go wrong?

CHAPTER NO. 6

I didn't know it was possible to get attached to someone in one and a half-day. But I knew now. Corner was more than just a formal friend to me. I had guy friends before. I have male friends in congress as well. There are people I've hung out with. But I have never trusted someone or felt close to someone as much as Corner. I trusted him. And I felt like we have known each other our entire lives instead of just a couple of days. It was a very weird feeling.

"Dinner's here!" He got off of the couch and went to open the door. Chinese food was here on which we both agreed on. It was my last dinner at his home. My house was repaired and the conference meeting was tomorrow. My wounds were healing fast and I was ready to take on the future.

He came back with the biggest and dorkiest smile on his face. "I can't wait to eat!" He exclaimed in a sing-song voice making me laugh. When I didn't know him I thought he was the darkest, mysterious, intimidating and rude person. And he was all of those things but not to the person who knew him. And ever since I came to know him,

I found out that he was the easiest person to talk to. He didn't make me feel weird or uncomfortable. And I was extremely grateful for it.

We dug into our food as soon as we unboxed it and it was heavenly. I realized even simple food could make you happy when you were eating with someone whose company you enjoyed. I was growing to very much like his company.

"Mmm, so good!" I spoke with my mouth full. He laughed looking at my face and we joked about the animal documentaries that we were watching on T.V. It had become our habit to watch mindless animal documentaries with zero volume on and comment on things we thought we understood. And I bet 50 percent of them were wrong.

We threw away the boxes after eating and placed the dirty dishes in the dishwasher. Currently, we were watching a documentary on tigers, and Corner was arguing about the scene that was playing with zero volume. It was some type of scene in which the tiger was running and suddenly he loses his balance and breaks his legs.

"I'm telling you Alexandria, the tiger breaks his own legs while running because he cannot control how fast he runs." He said assuredly.

"No! He did not break his legs because he was running too fast. He broke his legs because he tripped!" I pointed at the screen.

"What on plain grass?" He scoffed rolling his eyes.

"It's true. It can happen. People trip on the plain ground all the time." I said with indifference to his words. I was trying to prove my point that animals can also make mistakes.

"Yeah cause their dead ass clumsy. As you can see tigers are not." He said proudly. Boiling up, I grabbed the cushion and smacked it on his face. His eyes widened in surprise.

"How dare you!" He said with a laugh and a devilish smirk on his face. "You're lucky you're hurt right now or I would have pinned you on the ground and- "He stopped when he realized where he was going. His eyes suddenly turned from playful to dark and he stared at me with impeccable eyes.

"And what?" I urged him to complete his sentence.

"Let you go." He murmured. We were sitting very close on the couch and if I concentrated real hard I could see his pupils dilate.

"That's a great revenge plan you got there." I mocked. He smiled and turned his head away. And the documentary was long gone from our thoughts...

The clock was ticking 11:33 when we decided to finally head to bed. We both had discussed what was going to happen tomorrow and I told Corner about everything I was going to say in front of the media tomorrow. He said he fully supported me in every decision and said that he will bring all of the protestors tomorrow in the audience so that they can see for themselves that I was not in favor of the law. He said that they would fully support me too.

There was just one person I was afraid of offending and that was the head of the congress house, Benedict Wilbur. I told Corner about how powerful he was and how hard it would be for me to go against him because he is the biggest supporter of this act. Corner didn't meet my eyes throughout the time I talked about Benedict. I figured he was just tired and wanted to go to sleep, so I dismissed it. Corner promised me that nothing will bother me even Benedict Wilbur and I shouldn't worry about him. Corner suddenly seemed anxious and angry maybe because all the pressure was finally building up tomorrow. Hopefully, everything goes well.

We were currently heading for our beds to sleep. I slept in the guest bedroom yesterday after I forcibly helped him in cleaning it up. He said it wasn't used for a very long time because no one stayed over at his house. I could relate to him very easily because my guest bedroom had been locked up for years too.

Corner's mood was extremely off ever since we talked about the upcoming meeting tomorrow especially when I talked about Benedict Wilbur. I couldn't figure out how to cheer him back up.

"Corner," I spoke just before he was about to go into his room. He turned around and stared down at me. I think I was mistaken but I saw a glint of regret and fear in his eyes. "Umm, I wanted to let you know that I believe you," I said. His eyebrows creased in confusion, probably thinking what I was talking about. "You know...you were right about the tiger thing. He did break his legs because he was running too fast." And I saw a hesitant smile peak across his lips at hearing my words.

"Keep smiling like that." I murmured. "I really like it."

He again had that dark look in his eyes. But this time I swear I saw guilt flash before them too. But I couldn't figure out what he was feeling guilty about. He hasn't done anything wrong.

And then he said the most unexpected thing possible, "Would you sleep with me tonight?" I stared at him dumbfounded. "I- I mean just- you know sleep. N-not do anything." He stuttered making me laugh out loud. It was the first time I've seen him this hesitant.

"Sure," I replied. It was my last night with him together. And actually, I didn't want to sleep alone in the guest room either. I wanted to smell the scent which covered his bed and sleep in it like I did the first day I was here. He smiled at my reply and we both headed into his bedroom

I was already changed into my pajamas and he headed into the bathroom to change as well. I laid on the bed and relaxed into the now-familiar fragrance of him. His bed was extremely cozy. I could sleep in it for days. I remember the first I slept in it and stayed asleep for 14 hours. It was the most unexpected thing to happen in my life because I barely ever slept in. I laid on the left side of the bed and waited for him sometime. And I don't know when my mind drifted off into the unknown journey of sleep…

The sun woke me up the next morning. I squinted my eyes open and saw the blinds were open letting the bright rays of the sun, shine into the bedroom. I looked around and saw Corner sleeping peacefully. His dark hair was messed up and his parted lips and flickering eyelashes created a whole scene. He seemed like some character from a movie. And I was not exaggerating. He was extremely handsome and attractive. And I think he knows that too, that's why he is also showing off that devilish smirk of his.

I quietly got up and went into the guest bedroom where I kept all of my clothes that Roddick brought from my house. I changed into my usual formal dressing, white shirt and black skirt and got ready for the conference meeting happening at 10 A.M. I prepared myself mentally for the meeting as well. I had to be strong today for myself and the people. I just hope I'm able to pull all of this off...

~~~~~~~~~~~~~

I stepped down from the stage as the whole crowd applauded. The journalists were still shouting endless questions and the confused faces of the congress people tried to adjust everything in their heads. The conference finally ended and It was the first time I was proud of something I did. I saw Corner staring proudly at me as I delivered my lines and let the world know what I truly felt about this bill. The media was still shaking and the protestors were extremely happy.

I went backstage and took a few deep breaths calming down my racing heartbeat. I had to get to Corner and tell him how happy I was that I finally listened to my conscience. I peaked at the crowd from backstage looking at the seat of Corner. Surprisingly it was empty. I frowned and looked again. Still empty. Where did he go? I paced around backstage and tried to find him but he was nowhere to be found. The congress people were scattered everywhere and the angry looks that they gave my way didn't go unnoticed by me. I knew they would be angry at me for going against them but I had to do the right thing.

"You will regret this Alexandria." Mr Lockwood said in a bitter voice after approaching me. "You took the side of the protestors and now you're one of them for us." He said. "Don't come running to us when they betray you again. Your stitches didn't go unnoticed by anyone. Just you wait." He barked at my face and went away. I stared at him as he walked away. I knew I'd have to face all of this and I willed my heart to stay calm. Everything eventually turns out the way it was always meant to be. The people will keep talking and there is nothing I can do about it.

I finally went into the congress house and walked around the building. Corner was not picking up his phone either and I was getting extremely worried somehow. Hope he is okay. I passed through the office of Mr Wilbur and heard strange shouting noises coming from inside. I stopped dead in my heels and listened. I couldn't make out any word because the voices were muffled but I knew that both of the voices were male. I waited around for a few minutes, thankfully all of the workers and staff members were currently busy in the main hall where the conference meeting took place. So there was no one to notice my strange behavior.

I decided to creak the door a little bit open so the voices will come out. I knew the doors didn't make the creaking sounds because everything was well set in the congress house. And since the shouting noises were very loud they probably wouldn't notice the door cracking a little bit open.

I held my breath and slowly creaked the door just a little bit open, thankfully it wasn't locked. I saw Benedict Wilbur first, his face was fully red and he was staring at someone with that murderous glint in his eyes. I couldn't see the face of the other man since his back was turned against me but he seemed oddly familiar.

"You don't know what you're getting yourself into. This will ruin everything for you and for that pretty girl." Wilbur spoke and I frowned in confusion. He was always so proud of himself and he was really showing it to whoever he was talking to.

"No. You don't know what will happen when you pathetically lose in front of the Senate. I will make sure of it!" Wait a minute! That voice! I- I recognized that voice.

"Believe what you damn will!" Wilbur shouted in return and the other person finally turned around making my suspicion clear as day.

It was Corner Smith...

CHAPTER NO. 7

What the hell was happening?!!!

Corner?!

In the office of Wilbur?!

Fighting?!!!

I backed away from the door and placed my back against the wall supporting myself before I fell on the ground. My head was spinning. Was Corner hiding something form me? Why would he lie to me? Maybe it's just a big misunderstanding. I waited against the wall for him to come out and answer my damn questions. I had lived with this man in his house. Slept in his head. And after all the conversations we had about Wilbur last night, he didn't bother to mention he knows him?

I suddenly heard the door slam open and Corner came out with his face flushed red with anger. He closed the door behind him and then noticed me beside the wall. His face immediately lost all of its color and fear flashed across his eyes.

"Alexandria?" He whispered like he couldn't believe. "I-I was just about to meet you backstage." He said with his face pale as a potato. He looked like a thief caught red-handed.
"What were you doing in Wilbur's office?" I couldn't believe the voice that came out of my throat. I had never been this scared and angry in my life and I was sure he was hiding something from me.

"Can we talk about this over lunch please?" He looked at the closed door of Wilbur's office and then back at me.

I just stared at him like he was going to disappear in thin air.

"Please Alexandria. I'll explain everything." He said and pleaded with me through his eyes. I nodded and we started to head out of the building.

As soon as we headed out the door, my driver opened the car door for me but Corner insisted that I go with him in his car. I nodded to my driver and went to sit in Corner's car. It was a convertible and he had opened the roof. The fresh air whipped around my face and we both drove in silence.

After fifteen minutes we arrived at a restaurant and after five more minutes, we were settled into our seats which were quite further away from other prying ears of the people. I asked him the same question, I asked him after he got out of Wilbur's office.

"Alexandria, I can assure you it's not what it looks like." He started.

"Then what is it?" I said.

"After hearing everything you said last night I just got angry and I had to get it out on somebody." He said looking at the design on the table.

"So you just decided to go into his office and yell at him? How will that make a difference?" I was angry out of my mind.

"I know it doesn't but I just don't want him to go after you." He said looking at the table design again.

"Corner, you can't stop people from coming after me. And yelling at the most powerful person in the congress house won't solve anything." I told him. "Look at me damn it!" I yelled when he kept looking at the table.

The first thing I saw when he lifted his eyes was vulnerability. There was nothing else. He was scared of something. And it made my heart stutter for a few seconds.

"Corner... what exactly is it?" I asked softly this time, looking straight into his eyes.
He hesitated before speaking. But after a few seconds, he looked straight into my eyes and said, "I don't want to lose you Alexandria." He confessed.

It felt like my heart skipped a few beats at his confession. I tried to smile and reassure him that nothing like that will happen. But his voice had an alarming tone in it which felt like it was difficult for us to be together. I wanted to let him know that he won't lose me but I didn't want to make a promise I couldn't keep. Maybe something bad was going to happen that might drive us apart. I felt it in my guts.

"Why would you say that? Do you know something I don't?" I cautiously asked.

"I just wanted you to know that." He slowly said not meeting my gaze again. I decided to let it slide and talk about something else for now.

"Let's order something shall we?" I said to change the tense atmosphere and motioned for the waiter to finally come. We ordered our food and I tried to talk about different things to lighten the mood.

"So, what are your plans after this?" I said after the food arrived.
"I was thinking of taking a break from work." He said pouring water into the glass.
"Oh, so you can see your family then," I suggested because that's what I always did when I got a break from my work.

His hand stopped in mid-pouring and he placed the water bottle back down. "Yeah, I was planning on that." He muttered. "The food smells delicious." He suddenly said out of nowhere. The food arrived five minutes ago and he was just noticing how good it smelled.

"Y-yeah." I stuttered at his strange change of tone at the mention of his family but again decided to let it go. I will inquire about all of this some other time.

We talked about how the weather was changing and autumn was approaching. Turns out our favorite kind of weather is autumn and I talked about how I loved pumpkin spiced latte and he agreed. The day slowly turned into the light of early evening and we headed out of the restaurant. I let him know that I needed to go check my house and see if all the repairs were made accurately.

I got out my phone when it dinged to check my new notification. It was a message from Benedict Wilbur? I opened it and read the text.

TEXT: 'Meet me in my office at 6. PM. I have something important to discuss with you. Don't tell your boyfriend Corner aka Chris. I will be waiting patiently.'

What the hell?!!!

I looked up at Corner as he asked me if he could come along with me to visit my home. So many thoughts flashed in my head as I contemplated whether to tell him about the text or not. He would probably stop me from going. Or would definitely ask to come along. I needed some answers. And I knew Corner was hiding something from me.

Corner aka Chris? What was this? I needed to find out.

"I- Umm... have to go somewhere immediately afterwards. Why don't we schedule it some other time?" I said in a rush of panic seeping through my bones. I looked at the time. It was near 5 P.M. I needed to get rid of Corner so he wouldn't find out where I was going.

"So, we'll meet up later right?" He asked again, hesitant to let me go.

"Yeah, yeah definitely," I said in a rushed tone. I had already texted my driver to immediately come to the restaurant that we were standing outside of. I couldn't let Corner drive me right now. My nerves were too overflowing to handle his presence right now.

I looked across the road and impatiently waited for my car to arrive. "Alexandria?" He grabbed my elbow and slowly urged me to look into his eyes.

"Y-yes?" I stumbled over my words. I looked at his face but couldn't really focus on anything. My mind was in a haze right now.

"Alex." He softly tugged on my arm again to get my attention and I finally looked into his eyes. The fading light of the sun was shining over his head and the breeze was slowly blowing in the air, making my hair tickle against my cheeks. His eyes were asking me something. Something his words couldn't describe.

His hand came up to my cheek and he slowly brushed the tickling hair behind my small ear. The moment was so soft but my heart hammered in my chest. I shouted at it in my brain to calm down but it wasn't listening to me.

"I need you in my life, Alexandria." He whispered looking straight into my soul through my eyes. "There is nothing else I want." He confessed.

I somehow got lost in the depth of his voice. His eyes were searching my face and I could see the tension behind them.

His words kept echoing in my ear like a melody. *'I need you in my life Alexandria.'*

They sounded sweet to ears and I wanted to believe them. But the logical part of my brain was knocking on my fantasy door and I couldn't ignore it.

But maybe for one moment, I could shut it down.

He slowly leaned his head down towards me and I realized I was about to have my first kiss in years. I don't even remember the last time I kissed a guy because all I did was focus on my work.

Shit!

His eyelashes fluttered and he leaned a bit closer looking for my consent in my eyes. And I knew my eyes indicated I wasn't ready. I saw his eyebrows crease in puzzlement and he slowly backed away when he noticed I wasn't leaning in. I think he got the sign.

Just before he could ask me why I heard the horn of my car. The driver was here.
"Goodbye Corner," I muttered looking down at the ground and went to sit in my car while keeping my ears focused on waiting for his reply.

It never came...

~~~~~~~~~~~~~

"I'm not here to play games, Mr Wilbur!" I said when I saw him slowly pouring tea in his cup from the teapot. I was here to discuss some things not to take fucking tea with him.

I saw him chuckle at my words, keeping his eyes on his stupid task. That chuckle alarmingly resembled a chuckle I've seen somewhere else before. But I couldn't put my finger on it. His eyes were dark and deadly and there was nothing but cruelty in them.

"Why are you in such a hurry Miss Preston? I know why you're here." He said putting one cup in front of me and taking his own cup in his hand and taking a sip of his Goddamn tea.

"If you know why I'm here then I suggest you get to the point. I have somewhere else to be." I required.

He gave a dry laugh yet again, making my blood boil. "I can see he has some unique taste. Not everyone would want to get that close to you. You're a feisty little beast." He said taking yet another sip of his tea. I wished from the bottom of my heart that it was poisonous so he would die right now.

I sprinted to my feet at his last reply. I was not here to have some fucking tea time with him. "If you're going to play games then I should leave. I don't have time for such stupidity." I said turning around.

"You have plenty of time being played by my son." He said from behind. I stopped in my tracks and contemplated his words. Being played by his son? What the hell?

I turned around and stared at him to elaborate this stupid idiosyncrasy.

"You see Corner... I don't even know how he came up with that stupid name...is actually named Chris. And he has succeeded in playing more games with you than I ever have." He said coming around his table.

My heart beat rapidly at the mention of Corner's name. My Corner. The Corner which just confessed that he needed me in his life. This was unbelievable. This was the stupidest thing I have ever heard.

"I thought you were crazy but now I believe that you really are," I said, ready to turn back around because I was not going to stand there and be his little puppet that believed everything he says.

"I knew you weren't going to believe this that's why I bought proof." He said and took out a file from under a folder and set it on the table. My feet automatically came closer to the table and my hands flipped open the file. This can't be true. This must be some type of scam.

I saw his birth certificate and it stated that he was Chris Wilbur son of Benedict Wilbur. My eyes burned at the sight in front of me. "This can't be true. He is Corner Smith." I said.

He smirked and that smirked resembled Corner's. My eyes starting to sting. No!

"He also made up a fake surname? Clever boy!" He applauded. He took out a card and threw it on the table beside the file. "Is this your boy Corner?"

It was the identity card of Chris Wilbur. With his picture

showing clearly on it. My tears dropped from my eyes and my heart lost all of the warmth that had for my fake Corner.

This was the end...

CHAPTER NO. 8

So this was where my dirty fate was taking me? The dark prison cell of my ending thoughts. The person I thought I could fully trust tuned out to be the biggest traitor. My heart wasn't just shattered. It was burned and turned into ashes. And those ashes were slowly getting blown away by the wind. I was done with this world and trying to find the right one. I was done with trusting people. I was done with this whole concept that they called love.

I wiped my tears with the back of my hand as I exited into the lobby. I tried my best to keep my face down and positioned my hair around both sides of my face so people wouldn't notice.

I can't believe I was still so naive as to trust people so easily. Chris had been using me all this time to get revenge on his father. That's why he didn't tell me the truth about him being Wilbur's son. I fucking hated him with every fiber in my body. I was starting to fall for him. I was actually considering a future with him. And all of this was just a game for him. A fucking protestor who wanted to take revenge on his father and he used the support of a congresswoman to make sure he achieved the goal. How low could he possibly go?

I hiccuped and wiped my face again with the back of my hand. Tears blurred my vision as I stepped outside the building. There was nothing worse than a broken heart and I knew that now.

Without lifting my head, I went straight to my car as my driver opened the door for me.

"Alex!" I heard someone call behind me. That voice...

I turned to the right side of my building and saw him. Standing by his convertible. And now taking slow steps towards me. I looked at him with emotionless eyes for the first time in my life.

"Ma'am he has been following us from the restaurant and has been waiting outside the building." My driver informed me as I saw Chris approach me with slow cautious steps.

"Alexandria what's wrong?" He said coming closer. His eyes had that fake concern in them which I previously thought was real. "You left in such a hurry without saying anything. I was worried about you." He said looking down into my sore eyes.

I just looked up at him with hurt. So much hurt. This was the man I was going to give my heart to. This manipulative man who acted as he cared about me.

He noticed the tears brimming in my eyes and tried to touch my face but I backed away. I would never let him play with me again. "Alex..." He said. His voice just a whisper. And we both stared at each other without saying anything. This was probably going to be the last time I stand this close to him. Face to face. Eye to eye.

And so I did what I could never do again.

I slapped him right across the face with all the force I had in my shaking hands.

"Goodbye, Chris," I said through the lump in my throat and by the time he recovered from what just happened, I was already gone...

Six days passed...

I didn't talk to him. And I had convinced my brain that he didn't exist at all. But only till the time he called again. Twenty-five miss calls every day and endless messages. But I never picked them up nor did I read his messages. He also came to my house multiple times but I already told my security guard to tell him I wasn't home anytime he comes to the house. I wasn't going to let him make me a fool again. Not by his kind words. Not by his caring personality. Nothing would work on me this time. The only thing which I believed was that he was a liar. A big fat liar who didn't know how to clean up the mess he made.

I was inside my house staring mindlessly at the T.V. Some type of cooking channel show was happening in which I had little to no interest in. I wanted to watch some animal documentaries but some of my bad memories were attached to it. So I decided to watch something else instead.

My phone ringed and the first thought that came to my mind was that it was Chris calling again. I swipe opened the screen and saw that It was Roddick, my security guard.

I picked it up and placed it against my ear. "He is here again Miss. Alexandria." He said. My heart suddenly picked up its speed. But I tried to calm it down because I was never going to see him again.

"Tell him I'm not home," I said like I always did.

"He's not buying it anymore Miss. I've already told him multiple times." He said.

"Well then wait till he leaves himself. I don't want to see him ever again." I made it clear to Roddick and ended the call. I stared back at the screen and tried to get him out of my head. Failingly that's what I have been doing for the past six days.

Five minutes passed. No call came. I believed he might have finally left realizing that I didn't want anything to do with him anymore. He knew that I found out about his lie because I called him Chris instead of Corner the last time I said goodbye to him. And he should pay for what he did.

I suddenly jumped on my couch at the sound of harsh knocking on the door and the voice that followed behind was the most unexpected thing. "Alexandria I know you're in there!!!" I heard Chris shouting outside the door. Shit! I jumped to my feet and stared at the door in fear. "I just wanna talk. Please!" I heard him beg. Tears blurred my eyes once again. My heart started to melt down once again at hearing his voice. I clutched my hand on my heart and ran upstairs to my room crying my eyes out. "Please!" I heard his shouts from behind.

I knew the guards were probably dragging him away right now and it made me cry harder. How did it all turn so bad? I hated this!!! I hated this so much!!!

I opened the door of my balcony and peaked from it. He was getting dragged away by my security guards. One look on his face took all of my strength away that I had been building up for the past six days. Every ounce of my body leaned towards him even when I knew he was a liar. Is this what love does to you?

He was staring at my front door hopelessly as the guards pushed him away from my house. Suddenly his eyes turned towards the balcony on which I was hiding on and it was too late for me to back away. His eyes already found mine and I was glued in my place. Even from that distance, I could see the hurt and love in his eyes for me. But I reminded myself that it was all just a pretend. But his eyes said otherwise.

I thought he would scream at me or tell me to listen to him when he saw me but he didn't say anything. He just kept staring. I saw tears in his eyes mixed with regret and sadness. And it hurt me all the more. After a few more moments of staring, he turned around and left. Didn't scream, didn't yell, didn't beg me to come down like he did when knocking on my front door. He just left. Left without a goodbye...

Seven more days passed...

I didn't hear from Chris at all. Like no calls, no texts, no home visits. Sometimes I stared at my phone mindlessly while waiting for his call. But it never came. After he saw me standing on the balcony, he didn't try to contact me at all. Maybe he finally got the notion that I wasn't going to give him another chance. Maybe he finally gave up on making things right. Maybe he really was never serious. I kept thinking all of these things over and over again like it was my duty. I should think about getting over him not counting reasons why he left me.

I sighed and went in to take a cold shower to cool down

my thoughts. After the shower, I dressed in simple clothing since it was weekend and I wasn't planning on going anywhere.

It was 2:30 PM ticking on the clock. I decided to call my family and see what they were up to. I talked to mom and my brother for more than one hour. I told her everything that happened in the past few days just leaving out the things which were related to Chris. She told me how immensely proud she was of me for standing up against the law. And it made my heart warm just hearing those words. I ended the call with a promise to come to visit her very soon. I missed my family very much.

After ten minutes my phone ringed again. My heart leapt in my throat when I realized it could be Chris but I remembered that he wasn't trying to contact me anymore. I picked up the phone and saw the name of my secretary popping up on the screen. I swiped it yes and placed it against my ear.

"Hey Shelly what's up?" I greeted her. She was one of my oldest secretaries and somehow my friend too. She handled all of the important calls and gave me updates on the scheduled meetings throughout the week.

"Hey Alexandria, you have an unexpected meeting coming up." She said in a strained and tense voice. I immediately sat up in my seat at the sudden mention of a meeting. I wasn't scheduled for any meetings for this weekend as far as I remembered.

"This weekend?" I said frowning.

"No, actually it's today. I forgot to tell you, I'm really sorry. But a conference was going to be held today and reporters are also coming. You need to be there to answer some questions." She said in a rushed tone. My frowned deepened. A conference meeting? Today?

"What time?" I said.

"It's around 5:30 PM. You think you can make it?" She asked to confirm if I was going to attend. Maybe it was a good thing. I already didn't have any plans and I knew I was going to be thinking about Chris the whole time so I decided to take it as a positive thing.

"Yeah, I'll be there," I told her sighing.

"Good. I'll text you the address." She said.

My eyebrows creased in confusion again. The meeting was happening someplace other than the congress house hall? This was really unexpected.

"The meeting's not taking place at the congress house?" I asked rubbing my forehead in confusion.

"No, few of the congress people decided it would be best to take it someplace closer to the public so they would feel like they are part of the whole debate too." She said. It sounded so strange because she said the whole sentence in one tone with no emotion. I knew something was fishy but I couldn't put my finger on it. And since when did the congress people started caring about what people thought?

"Okay," I said and ended the call.

I had to be there to find out what was wrong. And my gut told me it was something really bad...

It was around 5 P.M and I was currently heading to the address that Shelly provided. I was ready and dressed in normal clothing. Since the meeting wasn't going to be taking place at the congress house, I decided to dress normally. The driver drove to the given address and we reached there five minutes early.

It was a normal-looking building, standing isolated on a street. It creeped me out how lonely the building seemed but I decided to put my interest aside and go in. The meeting has probably started already. The main hall was empty and strange looking. There was a girl on the receptionist desk who stood up as soon as she saw me.

"Hi, there! You must be here for the meeting. It's taking place upstairs in the main hall. Everyone's already there." She directed with a smile that looked way too forced and deep.

I nodded and said, "Thanks."

She sat back on her seat and I cautiously went upstairs to the main hall. Why did I get the feeling that something bad was going to happen? My heart thudded in my chest and I regretted not telling Roddick to come with me. I should have taken him here to this weird looking place.

I slowly went upstairs and into the main hall. And as soon as I opened the door to the main hall someone came up behind me. I turned around and the person muffled my scream with a hand on my mouth. Shit! I knew it was some type of trap! I tried to struggle out of his hold while screaming with my mouth still covered by his hand. He was strong, leaving me no place to escape. I tried thrashing my arms and legs to no use. And then I did the only thing I could do. I bit his hand. Hard.

He cried out and removed it from my face. I ran screaming and I heard my screams echo into the empty building. I hope the receptionist hears and calls for help. And then I realized that she must be in on it too since she was the one that told me to go up! Crap!

Before I could reach the stairs I saw another man running towards me from the right side of the hall also dressed in black. Both of the men's faces were covered in black masks making it impossible for me to know who they were. He grabbed me before I could descend the stairs and slammed my head against the wall. And the last thing I remember seeing was red...

CHAPTER NO. 9

I woke up to the smell of smoke. Thick, black, heavy smoke. That made it difficult for me to breathe. I got up with a heavy head and tried to keep my head low. The side of my head was stinging so bad and I cried out as I touched it. Black smoke was everywhere. Panicking, I ran to the door of the room and tried to open it. It was locked. I looked around for any windows but there were none.

Those men trapped me in here. The building was on fire. And there was no way for me to get out. I kicked and screamed at the door with no wail. Tears sprung in my eyes and smoke made it difficult to even breathe. I inhaled smoke with every breath and my mind was turning hazy. I screamed for help but there was no use. The door was getting hotter to touch by every passing minute.

I collapsed by the wall and tried to cover my mouth and nose with my arms. I would die from lack of oxygen before the fire burns down the door.
It was the end.

I patiently waited for my death. The fire was slowly

spreading all around. And every passing minute made me think of one particular person. There was no use in trying to ignore it anymore. I was going to die anyway. I loved Chris. I loved him. But my ending was already written in front of me.

How could I describe the feeling that I felt right now? It was not possible. Chris was nowhere to be seen and I was lost. There was misery everywhere. I saw fire all around me. Maybe this was the end of a beautiful beginning. And it was so weird. When you know you are about to die, you think only about the things which matter the most to you. And right now, being a congresswoman. Having the responsibilities of people and legislations on my head. My family waiting for me at home. My mother and my brother. But I didn't think about them right now.
The only thing I thought about and the only thing that I was concerned about was him. Chris.

The man who made and ruined everything. The building was on fire right now. And I was trapped inside it with no way out. And I knew I will be burnt to ashes till the fire brigade arrives because the fire was spreading quickly. I just had one regret on my mind. I should have told him that I loved him. I should have let him know that I cared. That after doing all the work of the day, he was the last person I thought about before I went to sleep every night.

But all I did was create hurdles, break promises and tell him lies. And now when I die, he will never know the truth. The truth that he has become the most important person in my life in the past two months. I lied on the ground breathing in the smoke from the fire. Living the very last moments of my life as my tears slipped away like my heart. I just hope he knows somehow that I cared. And I hope he knows that I believe him.

Flash Forward To The Present:

Chris's Point Of View:

I didn't hate my fucking life more than I did right now. Alexandria knew everything. And she blamed me for everything. And I was the dickhead that was responsible for everything that happened between us. She knew about my real identity and she thinks I'm using her for my own selfish benefits. My manipulative father convinced her that I was somehow just like him. Deceptive and merciless. But I was none of those things. And I wanted to prove that to her. But she wasn't giving me a chance.

I was currently heading to an address that led to an abandoned building. Why? Because I was stalking Alexandria. Yes, I have come to that phase as well. She wasn't letting me talk to her nor was she picking up my calls and it made me all the more worried.

The day that I pounded on her front door and begged her to listen to me, I became devastated as hell. She saw me from the balcony. Saw me struggling to gain her back. But she wasn't ready to give me a chance. That day before I left, I placed a hidden chip on the back of her car that showed me where it was. That way when she leaves the house, I would know where she is and wouldn't have to lose my mind with worry.

Right now I saw from my GPS that her car was placed in front of an abandoned house standing alone on a street. I didn't know what the hell she was doing there. I was fifteen minutes late because I was going away on a business trip out of town. But when I saw her car moving to some weird looking building on my tracker monitor, I immediately changed my route.

My heartbeat became faster every passing minute. It was like something bad was going to happen. Or has already happened. My palms were sweaty on the steering wheel even when it was cold outside. My mind raced with unwelcomed dark thoughts. I just wanted to see her and make sure everything was fine. I knew I had been worrying way too much about her ever since she found out the truth. And I knew all of these feelings could be false too. But I knew my soul wouldn't be at peace until I saw her.

For the past few days, she hasn't left her house that much either. She only went to the congress house then back to hers. This was the first time she went out somewhere like this and it made me incredibly anxious.

I pulled over on the street and the first thing I saw was thick black smoke rising up in the sky. My heart leapt in my throat and my foot squeezed the speed paddle with all of my force. I hit the brakes when my car reached the burning building and it screeched before shutting down.
It was the same building where Alexandria's car was

parked.

I slammed open my car door and ran towards the building. Her driver was nowhere to be found. I ran inside the building and saw the fire spreading around the corners of the front hall. One door was burned down right beside the hall. I ran and peeked inside it. There was no one there.

"Alex!" I yelled on top of my lungs. There were no other rooms so I went upstairs. The main hall was almost burned down creating the most smoke. I looked across the lobby and saw a small door which had just started burning. I ran towards it and my every step sounded like a heartbeat in my ears. My eyes were watering due to the thickness of the smoke. I kicked the door down and my worst nightmare came true in front of me.

She was there.

Lying on the ground motionless.

My heart strained in my chest as a bullet had just pierced through it. And the smoke wasn't the only reason that I couldn't breathe right now. I leapt towards her and gathered her small body in my arms. She was motionless as if she was dead and I didn't want to acknowledge it right now. I ran outside the room and out on the lobby. A burning piece of wood fell and ripped the skin of my ankle as I descended down the stairs. I didn't give a shit about myself right now. If Alexandria didn't survive, there was no point of my surviving either.

I ran out of the floor hall and finally got outside the burning building. I went and sat on the pavement on the other side of the road with her in my arms.

"Alexandria?" I couldn't find my voice. It was hard to address the girl that I might have already lost due to my reckless behavior. Her lips were purple and her face was covered in black dirt from the ashes of the fire. And I saw a scar forming on the side of her head like she hit it somewhere. But thankfully I got her out before the fire caught onto her. I realized my hands were shaking uncontrollably and tears were already rolling down my face as I examined her.
I took my cellphone out of my back pocket and called the ambulance. With a shaking voice, I told them the address and they promised to be here soon.

It was all my goddamn fault. Someone did this to her because of me. I should never have tried to get close to her. She was the one girl that intrigued me enough to puzzle my mind. The one girl that I wanted so bad that I could fight the whole world to get her. The one girl who I lost because I didn't know how to keep her and treat her right.

"Alexandria please…" I didn't know what I was begging for. I could barely hear my own voice as tears fell automatically. I held her tightly in my arms and wiped the ashes from her unmoving face. I could feel her struggling to breathe. She took in one small forceful breath after every five to six seconds. It made me all the more anxious.

I loved her. I loved my Alexandria. But she didn't even know that. And I was such a big massive stupid person to not tell her when I had the chance. She was all I ever wanted.

Few more seconds passed and she started to cough heavily. Her whole body vibrated as she puffed out smoke when couching. I held her close and smiled as happy tears filled my eyes this time. She was okay. She was moving. I took a deep breath and let her calm down.

She was still struggling to breathe but not like before. "Alexandria?" I whispered close to her. I saw her frown with her eyes still closed. She slowly tried to open them when she heard my voice. I could see she was struggling to stay conscious from all of the smoke that she inhaled. I kept my arm under her head to support it and waited for her to come around. She finally opened her eyes and tried to focus in front of her. I smiled through my tears as I realized I didn't lose her. She was here.

"Chris?" She said in a dry and weak voice. Her eyes were still struggling to focus but she recognized me.

"Baby I'm here." I held her face closer to mine. Making sure she knew I was here for her always. My life. My everything.

"Chris?" She said again like she couldn't believe it was me. My heart hurt in my chest and tears fell from my eyes as I tried to reassure her that it was really me.

"I'm right here, Alexandria," I spoke softly, brushing her hair back from her face. "I'm right here," I whispered.

"I'm sorry…" She said in a whisper before she faded away again.

I held her closer and cried, "I love you Alexandria." I said, wishing, praying, pleading, hoping, that she would hear it because that was the only truth I knew in this world. "I love you," I said kissing her forehead. I could not lose a precious gem like her. Never. My life would be over before it even starts. I couldn't imagine life without her anymore. And I will spend the rest of my time proving that to her...

CHAPTER NO. 10

Alexandria's Point Of View:

I knew where I was this time when I opened my eyes. Because this had happened to me before. I was in a hospital room. But at first, I couldn't recall why I was here. In the beginning, the only thing that came into my mind was the fire. Fire burning everywhere. But I couldn't recall where it came from. Then slowly the memories started to flashback in my mind. The call, the unexpected meeting, that isolated building, the receptionist, the stairs... and then...
Shit!

I was attacked.

I panicked and looked around my hospital room. I was alone. There was a beeping sound coming from the heart rate monitor, and it increased in speed and volume when I started to freak out remembering what happened to me. I tried to calm down but the horrible memories of getting attacked and someone hitting my head against the wall filled my mind. I hope they are caught. I couldn't believe I was still alive. I remember passing out after trying multiple times to open the door of the room in which they locked me in when the building was burning down.

And as if to answer my unasked question, I saw Chris open the door and come in. He stopped in his tracks as soon as he saw me like he couldn't believe I was real. I stared at him with wide eyes and an increased heart rate.

"You're awake!" He smiled and slowly came into the room. He gave a concerned look on my heart rate monitor when it increased in speed. "Hey…" He softly spoke coming towards me. I was on the brink of tears and was trying my best to keep them at bay. I didn't want to break down in front of him right now. I couldn't describe how glad I was to finally see him.

He sat down on the chair beside my bed and carefully touched my hand. And that was all I needed to cry out my fears in front of him.

"Alex hey!" He got up and came towards me, sitting on my bed and holding me in his arms. "It's okay. It's alright." He tried to calm me down, caressing my back with his hand. I cried out even more. I didn't know I was building up all of these emotions inside me until I got the opportunity to let them out. And it wasn't just because I was attacked and trapped, it was everything that happened in the past few months. The loneliness, the pain, more loneliness. It finally caught up to me.

And I remember when I thought I was about to die in the fire, the one thing I regretted the most in my life was not telling Chris that I loved him. I didn't care that he lied, I didn't care if he was true or not. I was tired of finding that out and calculating everything in my head. I just wanted him to know that I loved him. And my biggest fear was dying without telling him that.

"I'm here for you. It's gonna be okay..." He kept saying soothing words to me while trying to calm me down. He didn't even know that the reason that I was crying was because of him. Because I didn't give him a chance when he begged me to. I knew what that felt like now.

"Chris...I- I'm so sorry..." I cried wrapping my arms around him. I missed him so much. I wanted him so much.

"Baby... please stop saying that. You have no reason to say sorry to me." He caressed my face and wiped my tears away. I closed my eyes and silently thanked God for giving me a chance to make things right with him again. I felt comfort and solace in his arms. And I didn't know why I kept fighting with myself that I could actually live without him when in reality there was no chance.

"I should have listened to you." I sniffed. He held me closer and kissed my forehead. It sent butterflies down to my stomach because I had never been kissed like that before.

"You did. You always do. I was stupid enough to let you go that easily." He softly spoke. "I should be the one begging you to forgive me. I'm sorry." His voice vibrated a little, indicating how afraid he was inside just like me.

I looked up at him and immediately got drowned in his eyes. Those were the piercing blue eyes which captured my heart at the rally. Those piercing blue eyes that met me at the lake. Those piercing blue eyes that saved me from the protestors. He was always there for me. Even with a hidden identity he still tried to take care of me and be there for me when I needed him. I should have at least talked to him when I found out the truth instead of slapping him and leaving.

My mind flashed-back to a few broken memories when I was in the fire. I remember he was there. First I thought it was my dream but now I realized that he was the one that actually saved me again. I remember him calling my name, but I was too exhausted to answer back. And I also heard when he said loved me. My heart grew wings just imagining it in my head.

"Thank you for saving me," I said with great honesty.

He smiled, slowly showing off the adorable dimple in his left cheek, "I'll always save you. Because who else am I going to argue about when I watch the documentaries." He said making me smile too. Life seemed happier and easier with him. I closed my eyes and hid my face in the crook of his neck. My life was complete here. I didn't care about the future; I didn't care about the past. I was just happy in my present...

It was the end of November. Chris and I were walking to our favorite spot in the woods beside the lake. It has been two months since we've officially been together. After the fire incident was investigated, we found out that Chris's father was behind everything. He made up a plan and threatened my secretary at gunpoint to give me false information about the meeting in that isolated building. Two of his men were in charge of starting the fire and two others locked me up in the room. Everything would have been executed perfectly if Chris hadn't saved me. He got me out of the fire and reported against his father. After he was proven guilty, Benedict Wilbur was fired from the seat of Congress as punishment.

Chris and I remained together and got to know a lot more about each other after his true identity was revealed. I told him I liked Chris much more than Corner and he was quite happy about that. Mrs Wilbur was actually a really nice lady and most of my time was spent with her as well. And Chris's little brother felt like my own brother. Both of our families met each other and there were instant likeness and love which I was super happy about. Except for Wilbur. He still hated me and my feelings were mutual.

The bill was disapproved by the Senate after review and the congress didn't try to initiate it again. What was done was done. And now I had a very important person in my life with whom I could share all of my feelings and desires to. I wasn't lonely anymore and he was always there for me. He was the person I was most grateful for in my life.

"The sunset always looks beautiful from here," Chris said as we finally reached the lake hand in hand. This was the first place where we both met and I was starting to love it, even more, when I was with Chris.

"It does." I agreed, staring at the beauty of the golden light slowly fading in the sky. He looked over and me and smiled.

"How do you know?" He asked. I creased my eyebrows in confusion.

"Because I can see it. It's right there in the sky." I stated.

He shook his head and wrapped his arms around me so I couldn't back away.

"I said, the sunset always looks beautiful from here." He said and pointed at my face by touching my nose with his.

"You look like a beautiful dream turning into reality." He said holding me tighter. "My reality."

I blushed bright red. His eyelashes looked dreamy in the glowing light of the sun as well. "You're not so bad yourself," I replied. And he smirked showing off his famous life-taking dimple. I placed my arms up around his shoulders and rested against him. I wished in my heart that this would last forever.

"Can I tell you something?" I said looking up into his eyes.

"Yes," He nodded staring down.

"Remember when you saved me from the fire?" I started.

"How could I forget that. I almost lost you. It was hell on earth for me." He said and I felt his arms gripping me tighter. My eyes sparkled with so much love for this man.

"I heard it," I spoke.

"Heart what?" He frowned in confusion.

"You might have thought I didn't hear it but I did," I said to him.

His frown disappeared when his mind contemplated what I was talking about.

"You did?" He said in happiness.

"Yes," I replied. "And you know what I wanted to do after I heard that?" I teased.

"What?" He said eagerly. And smiled proudly waiting for my reply.

"I wanted to get up and slap you," I said. And his proud smile suddenly disappeared from his face. "And then kiss you and say that I love you too." I finished. And his smile returned again. He leaned down and kissed me passionately. I heard it when he said he loved me after saving me from the fire. And I remember I wanted to shout back 'I love you too' to him so bad but I was too exhausted to even move my lips. And then God gave me another chance so I could tell him.

He broke the kiss when we both became extremely breathless and leaned his forehead against mine.

Looking straight into my eyes he said, "I wanted to ask you something too."

"Yes." I nodded my head for him to continue.

He unwrapped his arms around me and moved two steps back. I stared at him in confusion. "Close your eyes." He said.

"Chris?" I tilted my head and asked him with my eyes as to what he was doing.

"Trust me." He spoke and I could see the nervous glint in his eyes.

I sighed and closed my eyes. This better not be a scare prank or something. I was already very scared of horror movies. I head a few ruffles of the grass like he was moving around and then silence prevailed until he spoke again.

"You can open them now." He said with a trembling voice and I opened them.

He was bowed down on one knee, with a black box in his hand. My heart jumped and I felt lightheaded. Was this truly happening? There was a glistening ring inside the open box but I had little interest in what it looked like. I couldn't keep my eyes off of the man who was bowed down on his knee right now.

"Miss Alexandria Preston, it has been an honor being your

company..." He started to speak, "the joy that I get when I'm with you, the smiles that we share together, I want them to last forever. I can't guarantee if everything is going to be alright but I can guarantee that I will be standing with you through every obstacle we face." His tears were visible in his eyes and mine were already falling down my cheek. "Miss Alexandria Preston, will you marry m-"

"-Yes!" I didn't let him finish the sentence. There was no need for it. He smiled through his tears and the box fell from his hand as I tackled him, wrapping my arms around his shoulders and sobbing uncontrollably. I was happy beyond words. And there was no one else but him that could do that to me. I didn't need anything. I just needed him.

He kissed my forehead and sniffed as his own tears silently fell from his eyes. "I love you Alexandria." He stated like it was the only truth he knew in this world.

I wiped his happy tears off with my hands, "I love you, Chris." I stated because it was the only truth I knew in this world.

He kissed my forehead and smiled, "Should I put the ring on your finger now?"

I laughed and nodded. He picked the box up and slowly put the ring on my finger. It was extremely beautiful. I didn't know a lot about jewelry but I knew It was one of a kind. A small heart-shaped crystal with blue and red hue inside it. It was extremely delicate and precious.

I looked up at him, "It's ravishing." I stated. "I love it."

"The blue and the red hue inside it reminded me of us. That's why I thought it would be perfect." He said. I smiled. The hues were intertwined together creating a beautiful sight.

"Your perfect," I said.

His smile widened and his arms wrapped around me engulfing me one more time. "Now that, that's settled. Should we go home and watch some animal documentaries, Mrs Wilbur?" He said with a happy smile.

I chuckled, "Yes Mr Wilbur."

And it was a beautiful beginning of a whole journey together. I didn't know what the path was going to be like, but I was sure we were going to make it work. I didn't have to worry anymore because I knew he had my heart and I had his. And that was all there was to know.

Printed in Great Britain
by Amazon